Slinky Malinki, Open the Door

Lynley · Dodd

PUFFIN

Slinky Malinki
and Stickybeak Syd
were a troublesome pair;
do you know what they did?
Alone in the house
one mischievous day,
they opened a door
and they started
to play.

They shredded a shirt
and they fought with a shoe,
a long woollen scarf
and a petticoat too.
THEN . . .

Slinky Malinki
jumped high off the floor,
he swung on a handle
and opened
a door.

They tangled the towels
and hung on a rope,
they paddled in powder
and slid on
the soap.
THEN . . .

Slinky Malinki
jumped high off the floor,
he swung on a handle
and opened
a door.

They tipped out some pillowslips
tied up in pairs,
they rolled up a carpet
and bowled down
the stairs.
THEN . . .

Slinky Malinki
jumped high off the floor,
he swung on a handle
and opened
a door.

They tattered some letters
and battered some books,
they scattered some paperclips,
pencils
and hooks.
THEN . . .

Slinky Malinki
jumped high off the floor,
he swung on a handle
and opened
a door.

They crept up on cushions
and vases of flowers,
they battled with curtains
for hours
and hours.
THEN . . .

Slinky Malinki
jumped high off the floor,
he swung on a handle
and opened
a door.

What a shemozzle,
the things that they did –
Slinky Malinki
and Stickybeak Syd.
They stirred up some spoons
and a bowl full of fruit
in a sea of spaghetti
and vegetable soup.

They knocked over packets
they went for a ride;
THEN came a scratch
and a rustle
outside.
So . . .

Slinky Malinki
jumped high off the floor,
he swung on the handle
and . . .

opened the door.

PUFFIN BOOKS
Published by the Penguin Group: London, New York, Australia,
Canada, India, Ireland, New Zealand and South Africa
Penguin Books Ltd, Registered Offices:
80 Strand, London WC2R 0RL, England

puffinbooks.com

First published in New Zealand by Mallinson Rendel Publishers Limited 1993
Published in Puffin Books 1995
Published in this edition 2012
001 – 10 9 8 7 6 5 4 3 2 1
Copyright © Lynley Dodd, 1993
All rights reserved
The moral right of the author/illustrator has been asserted
Made and printed in China
ISBN: 978–0–718–19543–4